Tides of Our Heart

A Second-Chance Romance of Love, Betrayal, and Redemption Beneath the Roaring Waves

Adegboye A. O.

Copyright © 2025 Adegboye A. O.
All rights reserved, printed in the United States of America. No aspect of this book is permitted to be used or reproduced in any area without written authorization aside from the element of short quotes embodied in articles or reviews where there is no best replacement.

Tides of Our Heart 1

A Second-Chance Romance of Love, Betrayal, and Redemption Beneath the Roaring Waves 1

Setting: A Small, Secluded Lighthouse on a Rocky Coastline 5

Prologue: The Return to the Lighthouse 6

1 8

The Encounter 8

2 10

Confrontation 10

3 12

The Unfinished Business 12

4 18

The Choice Between Past and Future 18

5 19

A Chance to Heal 19

6 24

The Heavy Decision 24

7 26

A Second Chance or Goodbye 26

8 29

The Weight of Trust 29

9 32

The Decision 32

10 34

The Heart's Decision 34

11 37

Stepping Forward 37

12	41
A New Beginning	41
Epilogue	43
The Lighthouse	43
About the Author	45
Acknowledgments	46

Setting: A Small, Secluded Lighthouse on a Rocky Coastline

The lighthouse is perched on a rugged cliffside, surrounded by wild, untamed nature. Waves crash violently against the rocks below, and the salty wind howls through the trees. The place is remote, nearly forgotten by time, but rich with haunting beauty and history. It was once a sanctuary for lovers, a place where two souls could escape the world and find peace in each other's company.

Years ago, this lighthouse was a place where the protagonist and their former lover shared stolen moments of passion and dreams of forever. But something—miscommunication, betrayal, or a life-changing event—tore them apart, and they've both moved on, only to find themselves unexpectedly drawn back to the lighthouse for different reasons.

Now, the protagonist returns to the lighthouse, seeking closure, healing, or perhaps even the chance to rekindle what was once lost. The arrival isn't just about revisiting the past; it's about confronting everything that led to their separation and the possibility of a new future together—if they're willing to face the truth of their past.

With this setting, the emotional stakes are high. The isolation of the location mirrors the emotional distance between the two lovers, and the physical setting—wind-swept cliffs, rocky shores, and crashing waves—adds to the intensity and drama of the romance.

Prologue: The Return to the Lighthouse

You stand at the edge of the cliff, gazing up at the familiar lighthouse. It looks almost as you remembered it—weathered by time but still standing tall and proud, its light casting a solitary beam across the sea. The sound of waves crashing against the rocks echoes in your ears, a rhythm that once brought you peace. But today, it feels different. The wind bites at your skin, and the air smells of salt and forgotten memories.

It's been years since you were here with him—years since everything fell apart. And yet, here you are again, drawn back to this place. Why?

You glance down at the letter in your hand. The reason for your return is clear. The letter—mysterious, unsigned—invited you here. The handwriting is familiar, but the words are cryptic. Was it really him? Your heart races as you feel a pull, something between hope and fear.

As the lighthouse's light sweeps over you, you hear footsteps behind you. You don't need to turn around to know who it is. The past has come rushing back to you in a single breath. The one person you never thought you'd see again, standing just behind you, is now here.

Turn around slowly, facing him for the first time in years, unsure of what to say.

1

The **Encounter**

You take a deep breath and turn around, your heart pounding in your chest.

There, standing at the edge of the cliff, bathed in the soft, flickering light from the lighthouse, is him. **Ethan.**

Your breath catches in your throat as you meet his gaze for the first time in years. Time has been kind to him. His dark hair is a little longer now, and there's a depth in his eyes that wasn't there before. His once-boyish smile has been replaced by something more reserved, but still unmistakably him. It's like no time has passed—yet everything has changed.

For a long moment, neither of you speaks. The wind picks up, whipping your hair around your face, but it's as if the world has stopped around you. Every nerve in your body is on edge. So many questions flood your mind, but the words feel heavy, stuck somewhere deep inside.

Ethan finally breaks the silence, his voice low and rough.

"I didn't expect you to come back here," he says, taking a cautious step closer. "But I'm glad you did."

You want to say something, anything, but your mouth goes dry. Your heart aches with the memories—the good ones, the bad ones. The way he used to hold you on nights like this, the way you thought you could make it work forever. But forever was a lie, wasn't it?

2

Confrontation

You take a deep breath and, without thinking, take a step toward him. The space between you both feels charged, electric—like the storm brewing just beyond the cliffs.

"**Why, Ethan?**" The words come out sharper than you intended, laced with years of confusion, hurt, and anger. "**Why did everything fall apart? Why did you leave?**"

The words hang in the air between you like an accusation, but also an unspoken plea for answers.

Ethan flinches slightly, as if the question stabs deeper than he expected. His eyes soften for a moment, his gaze searching your face for something—maybe forgiveness, maybe understanding. But there's something else in his eyes too. **Regret.**

"**I never meant for it to happen like that.**" His voice cracks, and for a moment, it's like the years between you fall away, leaving only the rawness of your shared past. "I thought I was doing the right thing... I was trying to protect you from something I couldn't control. But I was a coward. And I ruined us."

You feel the weight of his words, the honesty in them, but it's like he's only scratching the surface of something deeper. You want to believe him, but the bitterness of the past lingers too heavily.

The wind howls, and the lighthouse beam sweeps across the two of you again, casting long shadows against the rocky cliff. You can feel the pull of the ocean below, the same pull that once drew you both together—but now, it feels like that tide could tear you apart just as easily.

Ethan steps closer, his voice barely above a whisper. "I've never stopped thinking about you. About us."

For a moment, everything seems suspended. Your heart stutters in your chest as you search his eyes, looking for something you weren't sure you'd ever see again—**guilt, longing, perhaps even love**—but also fear. Fear that whatever happened between you two could never truly be fixed.

3

The Unfinished Business

Ethan's words hang in the air but don't feel like closure. They feel like an invitation to open the door to the past. But should you step through it?

As you stand there, face-to-face with him once more, you realize that so many pieces of your past are left unsaid. And now, you must decide how to proceed.

You feel a rush of emotion—the urge to shout, to cry, to throw it all away. But there's also the undeniable pull, that lingering connection that never truly faded, no matter how hard you tried to forget him.

Do you confront him with everything you've been holding back for years, or do you take a leap of faith, risking the hurt again for the chance at something more?

The lighthouse looms above, casting its beam across your path. The choice is yours.

Ethan's words hang in the air between you like a fragile thread, stretching taut with the weight of all the years that have passed since you last saw him. You stand still, your mind reeling, trying to piece together the fragments of memories that have been buried beneath anger, hurt, and silence.

"I never stopped thinking about you. About us."

The vulnerability in his voice catches you off guard. You had imagined this moment countless times over the years—what you would say to him if you ever saw him again, how you would demand answers, how you would never forgive him for what he did. But now, standing here in front of him, none of those prepared speeches seem to matter.

Your heart aches in a way you hadn't expected. The soft look in his eyes is both an apology and a confession, and despite the years of resentment, you feel a flicker of the love you once shared with him stirring within you. It's complicated—so much more complicated than you imagined.

The wind howls louder now, the salty air stinging your skin, but it can't drown out the deafening silence between you. Ethan takes another hesitant step toward you, his presence overwhelming and yet somehow familiar.

"**I didn't mean to leave like that,**" he continues, his voice full of regret. His hand twitches as if he wants to reach out to you, but he holds back, the distance between you both still palpable. "**I thought I was doing what was best for you—for us. I was trying to protect you from something I couldn't control, and I… I ran away. I thought I could fix everything on my own. But I was wrong. I've been wrong this whole time.**"

There's a rawness in his words, a rawness that shakes you to your core. The person standing in front of you is not the one who walked away years ago, leaving you with nothing but shattered promises. This man is different—worn by time, but still carrying the same guilt, the same ache in his eyes. The same love you once shared.

For a moment, you let the silence wash over you, absorbing his words and letting them settle in your mind. **You were once his world. You were the person he swore he'd never leave.** But then, in the blink of an eye, everything shattered. The trust between you both was ripped apart, leaving scars that have never fully healed.

"Why, Ethan?" you ask again, but this time, the question is softer, tinged with the aching need for closure. "Why did you leave? What was it really about? Was I not enough for you?"

The words hit him like a physical blow, his eyes closing briefly in pain. He exhales a long, shaky breath before speaking again.

"I thought I was protecting you from the truth," he says, his voice trembling now. "I couldn't keep you in the dark forever, and I couldn't face what was coming. I thought if I left, if I just... disappeared for a while, everything would somehow make sense. But I was wrong. I should have stayed. I should have fought for us."

Your heart twists as he speaks, and for the first time since you've seen him again, you feel the old anger begin to fade, replaced by something far more complicated—the haunting echo of what you once

had. The love, the passion, the promise of a future that was torn apart in the cruelest way.

You both stand there, caught in a whirlwind of emotion. The lighthouse, the crashing waves, the wild wind—all of it feels like a reflection of the storm inside you. It's almost too much to process. The hurt, the longing, the unresolved tension between you both.

"You think you can just show up and say those words after all this time?" The anger flares again, but this time, it's more of a reflex than anything else. You're not sure if you're angry at him for leaving, for trying to protect you from the truth, or for the way he's affecting you now. **"You don't get to just walk back in and expect me to forgive you like that, Ethan. Do you even understand the damage you did?"**

The words sting, but they need to be said. You need him to understand the full weight of the pain he caused.

Ethan's eyes flash with pain, but there's no defensiveness in them, no attempt to justify his actions. Instead, he steps closer, closing the gap between you, his voice quiet but firm.

"I don't expect forgiveness," he says softly. "But I do want the chance to make things right. I know I can't undo the past, but I'm here now. And I'll do whatever it takes to show you that I'm different. That I'm not that man who ran away anymore."

The sincerity in his voice is undeniable. It's not just words—it's a plea, a desperate cry for a second chance.

4

The Choice Between Past and Future

The wind whips around you both, the lighthouse's beam sweeping across the cliffs as if illuminating the crossroads in front of you. Do you let him back in? Do you allow yourself to open your heart to the possibility of something more, something that could heal the wounds of the past? Or do you walk away, closing the door on him for good?

Your chest tightens as you try to process everything. You can feel your pulse quicken, the raw emotions crashing over you like the waves below. You're not sure if you're ready for this, but the truth is—you never really stopped thinking about him.

You feel the weight of the decision before you. But you don't know if you're ready to face it yet.

5

A Chance to Heal

You stand there, heart pounding, the lighthouse light sweeping across the both of you again, throwing long shadows on the rocky ground. The choice is yours.

Something inside you knows that this moment—this fragile, intense moment—is a defining one. You can feel the pull toward him, the memories flooding back. You remember the laughter, the shared dreams, the warmth of his hand in yours. Those moments seem to rise to the surface, pushing aside the hurt, the years of silence.

You take a step forward, your voice barely a whisper.

"Alright, Ethan. I'll listen."

The words come out as a release, as if you've been holding your breath for years and only now, in his presence, can you exhale. You glance up at him, searching his face, needing to see that the man before you is someone who can understand the gravity of the damage that has been done.

Ethan's face softens as if a weight has been lifted off his shoulders, but his expression is cautious. The way his eyes search yours tells you that he knows this is only the first step, that there's a long road ahead—one that may lead to healing or more heartbreak. He reaches out tentatively, his hand hovering in the space between you before he pulls it back, unsure if the space between you is something he should fill just yet.

"**I don't know where to begin,**" he says quietly, almost to himself. "**I've spent so long regretting the way I handled everything, and now I don't even know how to explain it. All I can say is that I was afraid—afraid of losing you, afraid of the truth, and I thought leaving would protect you from all of it.**"

You nod slowly, trying to process his words. There's still so much you don't understand, but there's also something in his voice—a quiet desperation that makes you want to hear him out.

"**The truth, Ethan,**" you say, your voice steady, but your hands are trembling slightly. "**What truth? What were you so afraid of?**"

Ethan takes a deep breath, and for the first time since you've seen him again, he looks like he's bracing himself for something. His eyes meet yours, and there's an openness there, a rawness that you hadn't expected.

"**I should have told you everything from the beginning. But I thought I was protecting you from my past—from the things I've done. The mistakes I made before you and I met. The things I've been running from. And I couldn't bear the thought of dragging you into it.**"

You can feel your heart rate picking up as he speaks. His past? What could it possibly be? You'd known Ethan for years, and while you both had secrets, you never imagined there was something so deeply buried inside him that could cause him to walk away like that.

"**What are you talking about?**" you ask, your voice trembling now. "**What do you mean, you were running from something?**"

Ethan looks away, gazing toward the crashing waves below the cliff as if he's searching for the courage to continue. The air between you both thickens with the tension of his words—his admission—just hanging in the balance.

Finally, after what feels like an eternity, he speaks again, his voice low and heavy with guilt.

"I was involved in something I should've never been. Some people I thought I could trust—people I thought were helping me—ended up dragging me into something dangerous. It wasn't until it was too late that I realized how far I'd fallen. And the last thing I wanted was to drag you into that world, to put you in danger... But I couldn't protect you from the truth forever."

You're speechless. The realization hits you like a wave crashing against a rocky shore. **Ethan—your Ethan—was hiding something so dark, so dangerous, that he thought leaving you was the only way to protect you from it.**

Your breath catches in your throat, and your pulse quickens. A million questions race through your mind, but one stands out above all the others: **What happens now?**

You try to steady yourself, trying to find the words to respond. Part of you wants to pull away, to shut yourself off from this turmoil that is reopening wounds you thought had long healed. But another part of you wants to understand, to know the full truth of what Ethan went through, and maybe, just maybe, you'll find a way to move forward.

6

The Heavy Decision

Ethan steps back slightly, as if giving you space to absorb everything he's just told you. The weight of his confession hangs between you like a heavy mist, thick with unspoken words and the remnants of a past that neither of you can erase.

He looks at you with eyes full of sincerity and something more—**hope.** Hope that you'll understand, hope that you'll see the man standing before you now is someone who wants redemption, someone who's willing to face his demons if it means having a chance with you again.

"I know I don't deserve this, but I'm asking you to trust me," he says quietly. **"I know I've hurt you, and I can't take back what I did. But I'm here now. I'm asking for a second chance."**

His plea hits you harder than you anticipated. You stand there, caught between your feelings for him—the man you once loved, the man who broke your heart—

and the harsh reality of what you've just learned about his past.

The wind howls, and the lighthouse beam swings across the cliffs again, illuminating the path before you. It's almost like a sign—like the universe is giving you a choice.

7

A Second Chance or Goodbye

The wind picks up again, biting at your skin, as if nature itself is pressing in on this fragile moment between you and Ethan. The world around you feels like it's spinning faster, and your mind is scrambling to keep up, trying to make sense of everything he just told you. The past you thought you knew—the love you once shared—now seems tangled in a web of secrets and betrayals you never could have imagined.

The truth is, you've always known there was more to his story. Ethan had always been the type of man who carried his burdens silently, who guarded his emotions behind that quiet smile and those steady hands. He had a way of drawing people in, making them feel safe. But now, standing here, face-to-face with him after all these years, you realize that he was hiding so much more than you could have guessed.

Your mind races, the questions swirling like a storm in your chest. **What else is he hiding?** If he's kept this much from you, how can you trust him now? But then again, part of you knows that the man standing before you—the one who's looking at you with raw vulnerability, with regret and sorrow—isn't the same person who walked away all those years ago.

You try to steady your breathing, to clear the fog in your head. **You need time to process, to think. But there's something in Ethan's eyes that makes it impossible to walk away.**

His voice cuts through the silence once more, low and full of sincerity. **"I'm not asking you to forgive me right away,"** he says, his voice thick with emotion. **"I'm asking for a chance to show you who I am now. The man I am now. I'll wait for as long as it takes, but I need you to know that I'm not running anymore. I'm not the same person I was. And I'll never hurt you like that again."**

You stand there, feeling the weight of his words settle over you like a heavy blanket. The pain of the past lingers, but so does the flicker of something else—a spark of hope, of something you thought was lost forever. You've been living in the shadow of that broken relationship for so long, carrying the scars of it, that the idea of letting go of that pain feels almost foreign.

But could you really let him back in? Could you trust him again, after everything that happened? And what if this time, you were wrong? What if you let your guard down only to have your heart broken again?

As these thoughts swirl in your mind, you look up at the lighthouse again. The light sweeps across the sea, its beam cutting through the darkness like a beacon. It feels like a metaphor—a symbol of something lost and found, a light in the darkness, a chance to find your way again.

You know that whatever you decide here will change everything.

You close your eyes for a moment, gathering your thoughts. You need to know more, to understand the depth of what he's been through. You've always believed in the truth between the two of you, in the bond you once shared, but this truth is darker, more complicated than you ever imagined.

8

The Weight of Trust

"I want to understand, Ethan," you finally say, your voice softer now, a quiet surrender in the face of everything you've just learned. "I want to know everything. All of it. I need to understand why you kept it from me. Why you thought it was okay to walk away and leave me in the dark."

Ethan's face softens at your words, and you can see the weight of your questions hit him harder than anything else. His shoulders slump slightly, the weight of years of regret bearing down on him. He takes a deep breath, as if steeling himself for what comes next.

"It wasn't just about protecting you," he begins, his voice barely above a whisper. "It was about protecting myself too. I couldn't bear the thought of pulling you into something so dangerous—so far gone. But I was wrong. I should've trusted you enough to tell you.

The truth is, I was involved in something I couldn't get out of. People I thought were friends, people who knew my family... they were involved in things that I had no control over. Things that could have gotten both of us hurt. But leaving you behind was the hardest thing I've ever done."

You feel your heart twist as he speaks, and you listen intently, trying to absorb the full weight of his words. The danger he had been a part of—something so far outside the life you shared with him—was never something you could've understood at the time. But hearing him now, explaining his choices, there's a raw honesty in his voice that you can't ignore.

"And I didn't know how to come back from that," he adds, his eyes searching yours for some sign of understanding. "I thought I was protecting you from all the chaos I was part of. I thought I was saving you from the life I had fallen into. But in the process, I pushed you away. I abandoned you when you needed me most."

You can hear the deep regret in his voice, and it's almost too much to bear. The man you loved—your partner, your confidant—was part of something so much darker than you could have imagined, and he had kept it from you because he thought it was for the best. He had thought walking away would protect you, but instead, it caused both of you more pain than you ever thought possible.

9

The Decision

You stand there in silence, processing everything he's just said. The lighthouse looms above, its light cutting through the darkness as if to guide you, to offer some clarity. The waves crash below, a reminder of how far you've come and how much you've both changed.

Can you forgive him? Can you allow yourself to trust him again, knowing what you know now?

The truth of what he's shared has left you shaken, but it's also given you a new perspective on what happened all those years ago. You realize, deep down, that the decision isn't just about forgiving him—it's about whether you're willing to forgive yourself for the pain you've carried all this time.

Ethan's presence is a reminder of everything you've lost, but also everything that could still be.

His hand hovers in the space between you, uncertain but hopeful. His eyes search yours, waiting, willing to accept whatever you decide. **This moment could either be the beginning of something new, or the end of everything that was.**

10

The Heart's Decision

The air is thick with unspoken words, and the world around you feels distant, as though you and Ethan are the only two souls standing at this crossroads. The lighthouse's beam cuts through the darkness, illuminating the chasm that now lies between you both—both metaphorically and emotionally. Your breath feels heavy, your heart caught in a whirlwind of emotions.

Ethan stands before you, waiting for your response. His eyes, once full of mystery and mischief, are now open and vulnerable. He is no longer the confident, self-assured man who once left you behind. He is the man who regrets, the man who has carried the weight of his choices for years. The man who is begging for a chance to prove he is worthy of your love once again.

You feel a swell of emotions—anger, hurt, sadness—but underneath it all, there's a deep, aching tenderness that refuses to let go of what you once had. It feels like an old song, one that you can't seem to shake off. The melody is familiar and haunting, and despite everything, you can't help but wonder what it would be like to hear it again.

Could you really forgive him? Could you forgive yourself for holding on to the bitterness for so long?

For so many years, you carried the weight of that broken relationship, letting it shape you, letting it influence your future choices, your expectations. You told yourself you had moved on, that you had let go of the past. But standing here now, with Ethan's heart laid bare before you, you realize that part of you never truly did.

Part of you never stopped loving him.

But forgiveness is never simple, is it? It's not just about excusing the mistakes that have been made. It's about finding a way to move forward, to heal, and to rebuild something that was lost in the ruins of the past. The question isn't whether you love him still—it's whether you're ready to take that leap of faith, to risk your heart once again for the possibility of something real and lasting.

You take a deep breath, grounding yourself in the present. The decision before you is monumental. It's not just about Ethan, and it's not just about the past. It's about who you are now, and whether you are willing to open your heart to the future—no matter how uncertain or painful it might be.

11

Stepping Forward

As you stand there, time seems to slow. The sound of the wind, the crash of the waves, and the steady pulse of the lighthouse are all that fill the silence. Ethan's gaze is unwavering, his entire being focused on you, waiting for the answer that will define the course of your lives.

Your hand trembles as you reach out, but you don't stop yourself. **You step forward, slowly, cautiously.** Each movement feels weighted, like you're making your way through a fog, unsure of where you're going but knowing that you have to move forward.

Ethan's breath hitches as you take that first step closer to him. **He doesn't speak, but you can feel the tension in the air shift.** He's waiting. You're waiting. And for a moment, it feels like the entire world is holding its breath.

And then, you take his hand.

The moment your fingers curl around his, a rush of warmth floods through you. It's as if you've been waiting for this touch all along, for the connection that was lost, now found again. Ethan's hand feels the same—strong, steady, and warm. But there's a gentleness now, a tenderness that wasn't there before.

His eyes search yours, and in them, you see hope. **Not just for himself, but for both of you—for a future that is still uncertain, but one he's willing to fight for.**

"**I'm not asking for perfection,**" he says softly, his voice rough with emotion. "**I'm asking for a chance to show you that I can be the man you deserve. The man I should've been all along. I'll spend the rest of my life proving it to you if I have to.**"

His words hang in the air, raw and vulnerable. You can see the weight of the past in his eyes—the guilt, the regret—but also something else: the promise of redemption, of a future that can be built if you're both willing to put in the work. It's a future that won't be without its challenges, but one that could hold the potential for something beautiful.

You take a deep breath, squeezing his hand tighter. **You know the road ahead won't be easy. There will be obstacles, doubts, and perhaps moments of fear. But there is also love. The kind of love that once brought you together—and the kind of love that, if nurtured and cared for, could bring you back to each other again.**

"**I'm willing to try,**" you whisper, your voice barely audible, but filled with determination. "**I'm willing to take the risk... with you.**"

Ethan's face softens, and for the first time in years, you see a smile play at the edges of his lips—not a smile of arrogance or confidence, but one of relief, of hope, of something pure and real.

"**Thank you,**" he murmurs, his voice thick with emotion. "**You have no idea how much this means to me.**"

You stand there for a moment, just holding hands, letting the warmth of his touch seep into you. The storm inside you begins to settle, and though there are still unknowns ahead, you feel a sense of peace that has been missing for so long.

The lighthouse light continues to sweep across the ocean, steady and sure, casting its beam far into the distance, as if to guide you both toward something brighter, something new.

12

A New Beginning

The days that follow are filled with conversations—honest, raw, sometimes painful. You talk about everything: the hurt, the fear, the regrets, and the dreams you once shared. It's not easy, and at times, it feels like the weight of the past will crush you both. But you're both committed to understanding each other, to rebuilding what was lost.

Slowly, but surely, you begin to see Ethan in a new light. He's no longer the man who walked away, but a man who has learned from his mistakes and is determined to make amends. His actions match his words, and you find yourself trusting him again, piece by piece, moment by moment.

As the weeks pass, you and Ethan spend more time together, revisiting old haunts and creating new memories. The lighthouse, once a symbol of heartbreak, becomes a place of healing—a place where you both can look to the future, together.

There are still moments of uncertainty, but you both know that the road ahead will be shaped by the choices you make. And with each choice, you come to realize that love isn't just about the big gestures, but about the small moments—the ones where you choose to trust, to forgive, and to grow together.

Epilogue

The Lighthouse

Months later, you stand at the base of the lighthouse once again, this time with Ethan by your side. The wind has softened, and the air feels fresh and light, as if a weight has been lifted.

Ethan takes your hand in his, his grip strong but tender. You look out at the horizon, where the sun is beginning to set, casting a warm golden glow over the sea.

"**We've come a long way,**" you say, your voice soft but filled with certainty.

Ethan smiles, his eyes sparkling with the same love and warmth that first drew you to him all those years ago. "**Yeah, we have. And I'm never letting go.**"

You smile back, knowing that the future is still uncertain, but that you and Ethan are no longer afraid to face it together. You've rebuilt what was broken, and now, with the lighthouse as a symbol of hope, you both begin the next chapter of your love story.

The end, or perhaps, the beginning of something new.

About the Author

Adegboye A.O. is a master storyteller passionate about unraveling the mysteries hidden within small towns and tight-knit communities. With a background in investigative journalism and a keen eye for detail, Adegboye weaves intricate plots that keep readers on the edge of their seats. His characters are brought to life with depth and authenticity, reflecting his deep understanding of human nature and the complexities of moral choices. "The Silent Witness" is his latest work, combining suspense, intrigue, and the relentless pursuit of justice. When he's not writing, Adegboye enjoys exploring new places, uncovering local legends, and spending time with his family and two mischievous cats. He resides in a quaint village, drawing inspiration from the world around her to craft his subsequent thrilling narrative.

Acknowledgments

To the readers who dare to feel deeply and believe in second chances: this story is for you. You've shown me that the power of love, no matter how complicated or painful, is worth exploring. Thank you for letting me take you on this journey with characters whose hearts are as full of hope as they are of regret.

To my incredible support system: family, friends, and those who walked this path beside me. You've been my lighthouse through every storm. Your unwavering belief in me and my stories means the world.

To the lovers, the dreamers, and the heartbroken souls who inspire the tales of redemption, your stories keep me writing. May you always find a way back to the tides of your heart.

And finally, to the one who knows my heart better than anyone: thank you for your love, patience, and encouragement. This book would not have been possible without you.

www.ingramcontent.com/pod-product-compliance
Lightning Source LLC
LaVergne TN
LVHW061042070526
838201LV00073B/5150